W9-BRQ-073

STONE
SOUP

First published in the United States by Dial Books for Young Readers
A Division of Penguin Books USA Inc.
375 Hudson Street · New York, New York 10014

Published in Great Britain by Andersen Press Ltd.
Copyright © 1987 by Tony Ross
All rights reserved
Library of Congress Catalog Card Number: 86-16580
Printed in Hong Kong
First Pied Piper Printing 1990
E
15 17 19 20 18 16 14

A Pied Piper Book is a registered trademark of
Dial Books for Young Readers,
a division of Penguin Books USA Inc.,
® TM 1,163,686 and ® TM 1,054,312.

STONE SOUP
is published in a hardcover edition by
Dial Books for Young Readers.
ISBN 0-14-054708-8

STONE

SOUP

Tony Ross

PUFFIN BOOKS

The Big, Bad Wolf was taking a walk one day when he saw Mother Hen hanging out her wash.

He gazed at the things hanging on the line, and he had to admit that they looked very fine indeed.

"Hmmm," thought the Wolf, "there are goodies to be had here."

So he stopped for a chat.

"Good morning!" said the Wolf. "How about if I eat
you up and steal all your goodies?"

"Thank you very much," squawked Mother Hen.
"But wouldn't you like a nice bowl of soup first?"

"That's very kind of you," said the Big, Bad Wolf,
smiling. "First I'll have some soup, and *then* I'll eat you."

Mother Hen picked up a stone from the yard.
"I'll make Grandmother's favorite stone soup," she said.
"It's a very special treat."

"It must be," said the Wolf. "I've had soup at all the
best places, and I've never heard of it."

Mother Hen boiled some water and dropped the
stone into the pot.

The Wolf didn't believe you could make soup from a stone, so he sipped a spoonful.

"Peeee-eeeww!" he spat. "It just tastes like hot water."

"Of course it does," snapped Mother Hen. "It needs a little salt and pepper to bring out the flavor of the stone. While I season it, why don't you wash some dishes?"

"Okay!" said the Big, Bad Wolf, laughing.

When the Wolf had finished the dishes, he tasted the soup again. "Yeee-uccch!" he howled. "It's *worse!* Now it's just hot *salty* water!"

"Maybe a couple of carrots will help the stone to cook," said Mother Hen. "While you're waiting, perhaps you could vacuum the house."

"Okay!" said the Big, Bad Wolf, grinning.

The Wolf took another taste. "It isn't much better," he said.

"*Potatoes!*" cried Mother Hen. "Bless me, I forgot the potatoes." And she went to dig some up. "While you're waiting," she called to the Wolf, "you *could* bring the wash inside before it rains."

"Okay," said the Big, Bad Wolf.

Mother Hen let the Wolf taste the soup again.
"It's better," he said.

"But not quite right," fussed Mother Hen. "While I
get some turnips, could you just cut that into a few
logs?" She handed him a tiny ax and pointed to a huge
tree. "And by the time you're finished, the stone
soup should be just about ready."

"Okay," muttered the Big, Bad Wolf.

When the tree was chopped into logs, the Wolf took
yet another taste.

"It's fine," he said. "Let's eat it *now*."

Mother Hen took a sip.

"Not yet," she said. "A little barley will really add to
the flavor of the stone. While you're waiting, be an angel
and fix the TV antenna on the roof."

"Okay," groaned the Big, Bad Wolf.

"The soup smells delicious!" panted the wolf when he came down from the roof.

"Hmmm," sniffed Mother Hen, "there's something missing...errr...*mushrooms*, that's what it needs, *mushrooms!*"

The Wolf just stared.

"While you're waiting for the mushrooms to simmer," said Mother Hen, smiling, "you just have time to sweep the chimney."

"Okay," snarled the Big, Bad Wolf.

By the time the Wolf had finished with the chimney,
Mother Hen had thrown some beans, a little cabbage,
a handful of lentils, and a zucchini into the pot. Proudly
she gave the Wolf a taste.

He was delighted.

"Who would have thought," he sighed, "that a simple
stone could make such a glorious soup!"

"I'm glad you liked it," said Mother Hen when the Wolf had finished the soup. "And now you can eat me."

"I *couldn't!*" burped the Wolf. "I'm too full."

"Imagine that," said Mother Hen. "Then you'll just have to steal my goodies and get away."

All at once the Big, Bad Wolf leaped to his feet. He gave a terrible roar and then...

he snatched the stone and ran away.

Tony Ross

has written and illustrated many, many books. His first for Dial, *I'm Coming To Get You!*, won the first *Redbook* Children's Book Award and was named one of the year's ten best by Christopher Lehmann-Haupt of *The New York Times*. His other books for Dial include *Foxy Fables, Lazy Jack, The Boy Who Cried Wolf,* and *Oscar Got the Blame*, all written and illustrated by Mr. Ross; *The Knight Who Was Afraid of the Dark* by Barbara Shook Hazen; and *Meanwhile Back at the Ranch,* a *Reading Rainbow* Feature Selection written by Trinka Hakes Noble. Tony Ross lives in England with his wife and youngest daughter.